Home Is In Between

words by
Mitali Perkins

illustrations by
Lavanya Naidu

Farrar Straus Giroux
New York

In memory of my loving Baba —M.P.

To my husband, Satyam—partner extraordinaire, fellow immigrant, and keeper of my heart. With you, I'm home, always. —L.N.

Farrar Straus Giroux Books for Young Readers
An imprint of Macmillan Publishing Group, LLC
120 Broadway, New York, NY 10271

Color separations by Embassy Graphics
Printed in China by Hung-Hing Off-set Printing Co. Ltd., Heshan City, Guangdong Province
Designed by Mercedes Padró
First edition, 2021
1 3 5 7 9 10 8 6 4 2
mackids.com
Library of Congress Cataloging-in-Publication Data
Names: Perkins, Mitali, author. | Naidu, Lavanya, illustrator.
Title: Home is in between / Mitali Perkins; illustrations by Lavanya Naidu.
Description: First edition. | New York: Farrar Straus Giroux, 2021. | Audience: Ages 4–8. | Audience: Grades K–1. | Summary: Immigrating to America, a young girl navigates between her family's Bengali traditions and her new country's culture.
Identifiers: LCCN 2020018835 | ISBN 9780374303679 (hardcover)
Subjects: CYAC: Emigration and immigration—Fiction. | Immigrants—Fiction. | Bengali Americans—Fiction. | Home—Fiction.
Classification: LCC PZ7.P4315 Ho 2021 | DDC [E]—dc23
LC record available at https://lccn.loc.gov/2020018835

"Goodbye, home!" Shanti shouted.

She waved to Didu.
To warm monsoon rains.
And the green palm trees
Of her village.

The plane landed far away.
In a town with cold rain
And orange and yellow leaves.

Shanti clutched her parents' hands.
"Hello, home?" she whispered.

Their apartment felt like the village.
Inside was Ma cooking luchi.
Funny stories in Bangla.
No shoes.
Baba's big laugh.

But outside, town was strange.
New money to learn.
New manners, too—
Like napkins on laps.
No elbows on tables.
English words Shanti didn't know.

So back and forth she skipped.

Remembering the village.

Learning the town.

Again and again.

In Between.

Ma showed her how to dance Kathak.

Tonya brought her to ballet class.

Baba taught Shanti Bangla letters: *kaw, khaw, gaw.*

Shanti read him *The Little Engine That Could* in English.

Halloween brought trick-or-treaters;
Shanti gave out candy.
“Next year, join us,” Tonya said.
“Maybe,” Shanti answered.

Christmas came to town next.
At Tonya's house, Santa filled a stocking for Shanti.

Back and forth she ran.

Remembering the village.

Learning the town.

Again and again.

In Between.

Shanti danced through Bollywood films with her parents.

She laughed through Hollywood movies with Tonya and Malcolm.

For Holi, they called the village.
Uncles, aunts, cousins.
Splashed in paint.
Feasting on Didu's biryani.

They felt far away.

So Ma played the harmonium and sang village songs.

But later, on the piano, Shanti had to practice "Heart and Soul."

Back and forth she trudged.

If only her friends could learn the village.

If only her parents
could learn the town.

Again and again.
In Between.

Spring brought a surprise snow. Shanti and Tonya joined Malcolm's snowball team.

"You can throw!" a kid said. "Do you play Tee Ball?"

"What's that?" Shanti asked.

"Baseball, silly! Where are you from, Mars?"

Shanti didn't answer.

Suddenly, she felt tired.

Where *was* she from?
Village?
Town?

I need a rest, she thought.

So Shanti lay down.
Right there.
In Between.

After a while, she looked up—
At a blue sky.
With breezy clouds.
And birds winging by.
Watching over her village.
Watching over her town.
Watching over Shanti.

She stretched her arms wide.
She was good at making
anywhere feel like home.
Especially here.
In the space between cultures.

Now, home is in Between.

Shanti sings Didu's Bangla songs.
She hums "Heart and Soul" in English.
She invites Ma and Baba.
Tonya and Malcolm.
The whole town, if they want.

They remember their villages.
And dance with Shanti.
A Bollywood ballet.
Perfect—
For in Between.

AUTHOR'S NOTE

My parents were from the villages of Bengal. They brought me to the United States when I was seven and raised me in a town where we were one of a few families from other countries. I worked hard to understand "American" manners, slang, trends, and rituals—the "code" at school. At the same time, I was trying to stay fluent in traditional Bengali culture and language—the "code" of home. Going back and forth was tiring, and I often felt as if I didn't belong in either world.

But once I grew up, I realized that switching between two codes as a child had been a gift. It's like learning a new language—kids are faster and better at it than grown-ups. And if we work at it as kids, we keep some ability to crack cultural codes for the rest of our lives. "It's like a superpower," I tell young immigrants.

The space between cultures doesn't have to be a barrier; for children who grow up there, it can become a threshold of gratitude to celebrate the best of many worlds. Please make yourself at home in Shanti's story. Her name in Bangla means "peace."